Copyright © text Anita Hewett 1966
Copyright © illustrations
Robert Broomfield 1966
Anita Hewett and Robert Broomfield
have asserted their rights under the
Copyright, Designs and Patents Act, 1988
to be identified as the author and
illustrators of this work
First published in the United Kingdom
1966 by The Bodley Head Children's
Books, Random House, 20 Vauxhall
Bridge Road, London, SW1V 2SA
Reprinted 1968, 1970, 1973, 1975, 1979,
1983, 1986, 1989, 1994
Random House UK Limited
Reg. No. 954009
A CIP catalogue record for this book
is available from the British Library
ISBN 0370 00751 4
Printed in China

Mrs. Mopple's Washing Line

written by Anita Hewett

drawn by Robert Broomfield

THE BODLEY HEAD · LONDON

Mrs. Mopple was a farmer's wife,
and on Monday morning she did her washing.
"Now what have we got today?" she said to herself.
"A frilly pink petticoat
A pair of woolly bedsocks
Two white gloves
And a red spotted handkerchief."

Mrs. Mopple finished her washing
and pegged it on the clothes line
alongside the cabbage patch to dry.
"There!" she said. "Blow wind, blow."

8

Then the wind blew strongly over the cabbage patch.
Mrs. Mopple's Monday wash fluttered on the line
like flags in a row.
The frilly pink petticoat
The pair of woolly bedsocks
The two white gloves
And the red spotted handkerchief.

Mrs. Mopple went indoors, because she was going to get the dinner for herself, her husband, the pig, the turkey, the chicken, the jersey cow, and the rabbit.

13

Blow wind, blow. It blew so strongly that snap! went the pegs that were holding the petticoat. The frilly pink petticoat tossed in the air, twice round the haystack and over the farmyard. Then down it came on the little black pig, tight round his little black middle.
The pig sat down in the middle of the farmyard.

So there he was
A pig in a petticoat.

Blow wind, blow. It blew so strongly that snap! went the peg from one woolly bedsock. The bedsock went tossing into the air, twice round the haystack and over the farmyard. Then down it came on the gobbly red turkey, tight on his head like a warm woolly nightcap. The turkey sat down in the middle of the farmyard.

So there they were
A pig in a petticoat
A turkey in a nightcap.

17

Blow wind, blow. It blew so strongly
that snap! went the peg from the other
woolly bedsock. The bedsock went
tossing into the air, twice round the
haystack and over the farmyard. Then
down it came on the little yellow chicken,
tight round her neck like a winter woolly
muffler. The chicken sat down in the middle
of the farmyard.

So there they were
A pig in a petticoat
A turkey in a nightcap
A chicken in a muffler.

Blow wind, blow. It blew so strongly that snap! went the pegs that were holding the gloves. The two white gloves tossed in the air, twice round the haystack and over the farmyard. Then down they came on the jersey cow, tight on her horns with their fingers sticking upwards, like eight white finger-horns and two white thumb-horns. The cow sat down in the middle of the farmyard.

So there they were
A pig in a petticoat
A turkey in a nightcap
A chicken in a muffler
A jersey cow with ten horns.

Blow wind, blow. It blew so strongly that snap!
went the pegs that were holding the handkerchief.
The red spotted handkerchief tossed in the air,
twice round the haystack and over the farmyard.
Then down it came on the grey fluffy rabbit,
tight all over him spotted like the measles.
The rabbit sat down in the middle of the farmyard.

So there they were
A pig in a petticoat
A turkey in a nightcap
A chicken in a muffler
A jersey cow with ten horns
A rabbit with the measles.

So there they were!

Mrs. Mopple came out of the kitchen, and as she came
she said to herself: "Blow wind, blow. The wind has
blown my washing dry."
Mrs. Mopple looked at the clothes line, and as she looked
she said to herself: "Blow wind, blow. The wind has
blown my washing *off*."

25

Mrs. Mopple looked at the farmyard, and she blinked her eyes.
And as she blinked she said to herself: "Blow wind, blow.
What do I see?

"A pig in a petticoat
A turkey in a nightcap
A chicken in a muffler
A jersey cow with ten horns
A rabbit with the measles.

I don't believe it,
I don't BELIEVE it."

26

Mrs. Mopple went indoors to tell Mr. Mopple.
He didn't believe it either.
Do you?

28